BILLY BOT

• KID ENTREPRENEUR •

AND THE EVERYTHING LOCATOR

INVENTED BY LUKE SHARPE
DRAWINGS BY GRAHAM ROSS

THE EVERYTHING LOCATOR

WITHDRAWN

Simon Spotlight

New York   London   Toronto   Sydney   New Delhi

SIMON SPOTLIGHT

An imprint of Simon & Schuster Children's Publishing Division

1230 Avenue of the Americas, New York, New York 10020

This Simon Spotlight edition December 2016

Copyright © 2016 by Simon & Schuster, Inc. Text by Michael Teitelbaum. Illustrations by Graham Ross. All rights reserved, including the right of reproduction in whole or in part in any form.

SIMON SPOTLIGHT and colophon are registered trademarks of Simon & Schuster, Inc.

For information about special discounts for bulk purchases, please contact Simon & Schuster Special Sales at 1-866-506-1949 or business@simonandschuster.com.

Designed by Jay Colvin

The text of this book was set in Minya Nouvelle.

Manufactured in the United States of America 1116 OFF

10 9 8 7 6 5 4 3 2 1

ISBN 978-1-4814-6899-2 (hc)

ISBN 978-1-4814-6898-5 (pbk)

ISBN 978-1-4814-6900-5 (eBook)

Library of Congress Catalog Card Number 2015950427

Chapter One

Ultra-Cheesy Lasagna

MY NAME IS BILLY SURE. I'M THIRTEEN YEARS OLD. I'm also a seventh grader at Fillmore Middle School and—oh yeah, I just got home from a busy day at the office.

At the office? you might ask. Along with my best friend, Manny Reyes, who runs the business stuff while I invent, we run the invention company **SURE THINGS, INC.** Sure Things, Inc. has come out with all kinds of cool inventions you've probably heard of, including the **ALL BALL**, the **SIBLING SILENCER**, and our latest creation, the **MAGICAL MICROPHONE**.

"Well, you're home early for a change," Mom says as I walk into the kitchen.

"Yeah, it's kind of in-between time for Manny and me," I explain. "We're still testing out the Magical Microphone, and the REALLY GREAT HOVERCRAFT TOY and the INVISIBILITY KIT are just hitting stores now, so the pressure is off for the moment to invent something new."

"Great!" says Mom. "Then you can help me set the table for dinner."

As I help Mom put out plates, silverware, napkins, and cups, I think about how great it has been having her home for so long. My mom spends a lot of time away for work. You know how my job as an inventor is cool? My mom has a cool job too—she's a spy! She protects the whole country. Although she's home now, she can be called into a spy mission at any time. So I'm thankful just to have her here.

My dad is an artist. He paints all kinds of, um, "unique" things. Like my dog Philo's nostrils, whiskers, and butt. He recently put up all his work in an art gallery and it was a big success.

So Fancy!

Oh no—that's when I remember. Dad's art gallery. Not too long ago I overheard a conversation between my mom and dad, though I don't think they know I heard them. An art lover offered Dad a job to paint for her—all the way in Italy!

I know, I know. I should be really happy for him. But if Dad is away, and Mom suddenly gets called off to save the world, who will take care of my sister, Emily, and me?

"You're awfully quiet tonight, Billy," Mom says.

"Yeah," I say, placing a fork on the table. What can I say? I can't let on that I overheard Mom and Dad's conversation.

Mom is unfazed.

"Well, I know something that will perk you right up—tonight's dinner," she says. "We're having the Sure family secret ultra-cheesy lasagna recipe!"

"THE SURE FAMILY SECRET ULTRA-CHEESY LASAGNA RECIPE?" I ask.

I think after living in this house for thirteen years I would know if there was a Sure family secret ultra-cheesy lasagna recipe!!!

"Oh, well, you may know it by a different name," Mom says. I can see a sly grin spreading across her face. "Takeout."

Okay, now *that* I know. Normally I would

get a kick out of Mom's little joke. I'd also be super psyched about eating takeout, especially Italian food takeout. But the fact it's, well, *Italian*, makes me nervous. Is tonight the night we find out Dad is moving to Italy?

A few minutes later Dad and Emily join Mom and me at the table.

I immediately notice that Emily is not wearing a hat.

If this sounds strange to you, let me explain. My sister always has a "thing"—something she gets into, like wearing giant hats or talking in a British accent—that is absolutely the 100 percent most important thing in the whole wide world to her at the time. Emily's things come from nowhere. And then they fade into nowhere fast.

So seeing Emily hatless? That means her next thing will reveal itself soon.

I can hardly wait.

The meal proceeds quietly, and my thoughts turn to an upcoming meeting of the Fillmore Middle School Inventors Club. I started the club and kind of stepped back when things got extra busy at Sure Things, Inc. But I really like the way club has become a place for kids to hang out and test their inventing skills at my school.

I'm thinking about going to the next meeting when Dad speaks up.

"I have an announcement to make," he says.

I stop chewing.

Oh no. This is it.

"As Emily learned by writing thank-you notes to everyone who came to the art exhibit, my show was a success," Dad says. "In fact, it was so successful that an art dealer in Italy named Tali DeCiso contacted me and asked me to do a series of paintings for her!"

I put my fork down, feeling sick, just as Emily squeals.

"That is so fantastic, Dad!" says Emily. "It's amazing! And to think, that happened because of the thank-you note I wrote."

"Um, I think your father's paintings had a

little something to do with it as well, Emily," Mom points out.

"It's really a once in a lifetime opportunity," says Dad.

This is it. Here it comes. Dad's big announcement that he's moving to Italy.

"Your mom and I have talked it over, and we've come to the conclusion . . ."

Dad pauses. I brace myself for the worst.

"The ENTIRE SURE FAMILY is moving to Italy!"

Chapter Two

The Big Announcement

OKAY, *THIS* I WAS NOT READY FOR. MY JAW DROPS. IN fact, if it dropped any farther, I'd be in danger of hitting the dust bunnies on the floor under the dining room table.

The entire Sure family is moving to Italy? I'm moving to Italy?

Still unable to speak, I look over at Emily. She can't be happy about this. She's never happy about change. But . . . as I look over, I wonder, is my sister *smiling?*

In addition to smiling, she's counting on her fingers, like she's trying to solve a math problem in her head. Then I watch her type Gemma Weston's name into her phone. Gemma is a British celebrity. Oh yeah, she's also one of Emily's good friends.

"So Italy is, what? Like a two-hour flight from England?" she asks.

Mom and Dad nod.

"So that means that we'd be much closer to Gemma once she flies back home to England," Emily says triumphantly. "And we'd also be close to all her celebrity friends. This is fantastic! Great idea, Dad!"

Celebrity friends

"I'm thinking about all the fresh super-yummy lasagna we'll get to eat," Mom adds enthusiastically, shoveling a garlic roll into her mouth.

What is going on here?! How is everyone okay with this?

I finally find my voice. "But . . . what about SCHOOL?" I ask. It's the first thing I can think of.

"We thought about that," says Dad. "We'll arrange for Italian and English language tutors for both of you. It's pretty common for American families living abroad."

"THE INVENTORS CLUB?" I ask in a small voice, realizing that maybe this isn't the most compelling argument.

"Isn't Clayton Harris doing a great job running the club?" Mom says.

"Well, yeah, he is, but I mean, I still go to meetings and I like to feel like part of it, and . . ." My sentence trails off as I realize what is really troubling me about this move. It isn't school or the inventor's club. It's . . .

"SURE THINGS, INC.?" I ask. "MANNY?"

There, I said it. I can go to school anywhere, and Clayton can run the club without me. But how can there be a Sure Things, Inc. without Billy Sure? How can Manny and I be a team without, well, our team?

To my surprise, Emily speaks up.

"Dad just got a really big break," she says to me. "Potentially the biggest break of his art career, and all you can think about is yourself?"

"Well, I—"

But she's not done.

"You should be happy for him," Emily says to me. "Not whining about what you'll miss."

I suddenly feel a little embarrassed. I know I should feel happy for Dad, but . . .

Mom walks over to my chair and gives me a hug. Sometimes it's like she can read my mind.

"We all know how important Manny and Sure Things, Inc. are to you, Billy," she says. "They're important to us, too. We'll make sure that you have the best webcams available to stay in touch with Manny every day. After all, you and Abby made the Sibling Silencer together over a webcam and did a fantastic job."

Well, that's true. But I didn't know Abby. Working with Manny is a whole other thing. He's not just my business partner. He's my best friend!

But what can I do? I don't want to be the one who causes a family problem. I don't want to be the selfish one. I have no choice. I guess I'm moving to Italy.

"Okay," I say finally. Even I can hear the lack of enthusiasm in my voice.

"Great!" says Dad, caught up in his own excitement. "We're leaving in two weeks!"

Wait. What? Two weeks. TWO WEEKS?!

How am I going to get ready? How am I going to set things up for while I'm gone? How am I going to pack?

How am I going to tell Manny?!

After dinner I head to my room. I try hard to get some homework done, but I can't concentrate. I usually get this way when I'm struggling to finish an invention. But I have no idea how to deal with *this*.

Finally, unable to really get anything done, I put my homework aside. As I walk toward my bed I spot a framed photo on my shelf. It's a shot of Manny and me with my baseball hero, Carl Bourette, on the **Better Than Sleeping!** TV show shortly after the All Ball came out.

I pick up the photo and stare at it for a few minutes. Just looking at the picture makes me feel sad. What will happen to Sure Things, Inc. while I'm in Italy? Will we ever have another successful invention? Is Sure Things, Inc. DOOMED?

I fall asleep that night and slip into a crazy dream. I'm standing on top of the Leaning Tower of Pisa, except it's made entirely of spaghetti. Oh, and it's raining parmesan cheese and it's also snowing chunks of gelato. . . .

"Manny! Manny! Can you hear me back in America?" I yell.

Tourists start to gather below, looking up
and wondering why I'm shouting. A man takes
a picture of me.

"Manny, I have a great idea for an invention!" I yell, louder now. I wave my arms up
and down, frantically trying to contact Manny.

And then, just as I raise my arms again, I
slip and fall off the tower!!

I plunge toward the ground below as horrified onlookers scream and point up at me.

"AAAAAAAAH!!!!!!"

Just before I hit the ground, I wake up.

And then I remember that today is the day I have to tell Manny about the move.

In school I try my best to focus on my classes. They actually do help a bit to distract me. Although talking about Roman myths in English class doesn't really help!

I see Manny at lunch. I could tell him now about the move, but it might be best to wait until school is over and we're at the office. We don't say much to each other at lunch, which I think suits Manny just fine. He's busy looking up sales figures for our inventions anyway.

On my way to my last class I hear a familiar voice call out to me.

"Billy!"

It's Clayton Harris, the president of the inventors club.

"Hi, Clayton, what's up?" I say, trying to sound as casual as possible.

"I want to show you the improvements I've made on my latest invention," he says. "Do you have some time after school today?"

"I'm sorry, Clayton," I say. "I really have to get to the office right away after school. I have to tell . . . I have some important things to discuss with Manny. Can we do it another time?"

"Of course, Billy," Clayton says, smiling. "Sure Things, Inc. comes first! See you."

"Thanks," I say, then I head to my last class. *Sure Things, Inc. comes first!*

After school it's go time. I can't put it off any longer. I need to talk to Manny. I stop at home, grab a snack, pick up Philo, and bike to the World Headquarters of Sure Things, Inc., which just so happens to be located in Manny's garage. This trip, which I've made hundreds of times, feels EXTRA SPECIAL today.

I walk through the office door and find Manny scanning a spreadsheet of marketing plans, like he does every day.

It hits me. How many more times am I going to bike over here and find him like that?

Images of me and Manny working together in this office race through my mind. I think of all the great things we could invent—and all the fun we'll miss out on together. What if that never happens again?

Just as I'm crafting a delicate, intricate way to break the news to Manny, he turns to me.

"What's up, partner?" he asks in his cheery Manny way.

"Manny," I say. I can't help it. I'm going to blurt it all out! "I'm moving to Italy in THIR-TEEN DAYS!"

Chapter Three

Decisions and Solutions

"ITALY, HUH?" MANNY SAYS, AS CASUALLY AS IF I HAD just suggested that we eat burritos for lunch, or perhaps that we switch to more energy-efficient lightbulbs in the office. "Sounds like there's a story here."

I almost laugh. Manny is so calm, it nearly puts me at ease—reason #368 why I'm glad he's my best friend and business partner. That's going to make me miss him even more.

I quickly fill Manny in on Tali DeCiso and the rest of the details.

"What does Emily think about all of this?"

Manny asks, the corner of his mouth curling into a small, sly smile.

"Are you kidding? She loves it! Italy is only a two-hour flight from England, where Gemma lives. She's all excited about meeting Gemma's celebrity pals."

"Hmm," Manny says, scratching the side of his head.

Manny swivels his chair back around to face his computer screen and quickly pulls up Tali DeCiso's website. It's a real website all right—filled with tons of reblogged images of paintings, each one as kooky as Dad's. In fact, Dad's painting of Philo's butt is featured prominently on the homepage.

"She's quite the art collector," Manny says.

The homepage has paintings of doorknobs, windshield wipers, donut crumbs, and some really gross-looking goopy food. I guess I know now why Tali DeCiso likes Dad's work so much.

"Here's a close-up of someone's nostril," Manny says, hovering over another image.

"I was wondering what that was," I admit. "You know, Manny, it kinda looks likes *your* nostril."

We both crack up.

"I guess we have to talk about what happens to Sure Things, Inc. while I'm in Italy," I say, finally bringing up the necessary but unpleasant topic. "My mom told me that I'll have a state-of-the-art webcam so we can talk every day over video chat."

"That makes sense," Manny says, nodding.

"But Sure Things, Inc. just won't feel the same," I say. "I can't imagine not working beside you, here in person."

"It's obviously not ideal, but we can make it work," Manny assures me. "We could brainstorm, have meetings, talk about what we are each working on. . . ."

"I know that lots of companies have offices all over the world and have web meetings every day," I say. "I just worry that inventing for Sure Things, Inc. will become more like any other job than the fun adventure it's been so far."

For a second there it seems as if Manny *isn't* listening to what I'm saying. But I know him better than that. He's heard me and is already concocting some elaborate plan to make every-thing all better.

Okay, not *all* better, but at least a way to find something positive.

"I HAVE AN IDEA," Manny says.

See?

"Why don't we work on a last hurrah proj-ect as a team, here in the office?" he asks. "You know, musicians do it. When they release their last album or go on their final tour together, they make a big deal about it being their LAST HURRAH. It really gets everyone excited. Everyone wants to buy the last album or see them in that final concert."

"Okay . . . ," I say, feeling a little dense that I'm not exactly sure where this is going.

"We can do the same thing with an invention!" Manny says, finally getting to the point. "One last, real Sure Things, Inc. invention. And it won't be *that* sad. It's not like we won't be working together at all. It'll just be the last time we work the way we always have. What do you think?"

I think for a moment. It could be really fun to crank out a new invention with Manny. It might even help to take my mind off what's about to happen, and it could make my final two weeks here fun and memorable.

"I like it!" I say, trying to muster the biggest smile I can.

"Great!" Manny says. "Now we just need a fabulous idea."

"Right. Which at the moment, we don't have."

We both laugh. I'm happy that Manny has

managed to brighten up even this sad situation.

"Time to brainstorm!" Manny says, rubbing his hands together. "RAPID-FIRE STYLE. Whatcha got?"

"Well, how about . . . let's see . . . oh, I know. A LUNCHBOX IDENTIFIER," I suggest. I don't know where that one came from. It just popped into my head.

"Okay," Manny says, sounding cautious. "And what's it do?"

"It would scan everyone's lunchbox in the school before lunchtime and tell you exactly what each person brought for lunch that day," I explain. "That way you would know who to sit next to. It could be popular for kids who don't like the smell of egg salad or are allergic to specific ingredients."

"Hmm," says Manny.

I know that particular "hmm." That's Manny's "I want to be polite and not hurt Billy's feelings but I really don't think this is a very good idea" hmm.

"I don't see a really huge demand for that one, Billy," he says. "Kids will want to sit with their friends anyway, not with who brought whatever for lunch."

"Right, right," I say. "Good point. Okay, how about PIZZA IN A CAN? All you have to do for a fresh slice of pizza is open up a can!"

This might actually be a good idea.

"But if you're buying a can of pizza already, wouldn't you just buy a pizza?" Manny asks.

Or not such a good idea.

"Okay, I can't force a good idea to happen," I admit. "What if I get a jump start on my math homework? I always get distracted when I do my math homework, so maybe my brain will come up with a brilliant idea for an invention while I'm supposed to be working."

Manny nods and turns back to his spreadsheets.

But after an hour staring at my textbook, the only amazing thing that's happened is that I've managed to complete my math homework. No luck with invention ideas!

"Let me think about it some more tonight," I say. I always do my best invention brainstorming at night, often while I'm sleeping! I gather up my stuff, place my math homework carefully in my backpack, and head home.

That night at dinner everyone is in a pretty good mood, which is surprising because my dad cooked. (He might be an okay painter, but he is definitely *not* a good chef.) Today's dinner is "eggplant surprise," so Emily, Mom, and I use plenty of GROSS-TO-GOOD POWDER, an invention that we keep in the saltshaker and makes bad food taste delicious.

"I've been looking at some of the latest Italian fashions," Mom admits as she dives into some of the surprise. (I think the surprise is a raw onion.) "I can't wait to shop in those adorable boutiques."

That reminds me—Mom loves weird little thrift stores.

"I think that being in a place so different from home will inspire all kinds of new paintings for me," says Dad.

Emily swallows the bite of dinner she was chewing.

"Dad, your eggplant surprise tastes wonderful, like *scarpa*." She has an Italian-English dictionary on her lap.

"Thanks, honey," says Dad, "but '*scarpa*' means 'shoe.'" (Dad studied Italian in college.)

"Oh. Well, the Italian language is still *arancia* to me. But I'm studying," Emily says.

"Um . . . actually what you just said is that the Italian language is still 'orange' to you," says Dad. "But you keep studying, Em."

I smile. Using random, incorrect Italian words in sentences?

That sounds like Emily's new thing, all right!

After dinner I head up to my room.

"Have an *ananas* night, Billy," Emily tells me cheerfully.

"Thanks, Em," I say, though it doesn't stop me from looking up the word *"ananas"* when I reach my room. It means "pineapple."

In so many ways, this is going to be a long two weeks.

Or now—twelve days!

Chapter Four

Location, Location, Location!

I'M IN ITALY AGAIN, THIS TIME WANDERING THE streets. I pass cafés where people sit and munch on cannoli. Some of them share tiramisu.

I walk around a street corner and I'm suddenly standing in front of the Colosseum of Rome. Only it's not the Colosseum as it is today—it's the Colosseum of *Ancient Rome!* I can hear the sounds of ancient gladiators clashing.

Just then a man wearing a toga comes up to me and starts speaking in Italian very fast.

"I'm sorry," I admit. "I don't speak Italian! I don't know what you're saying!"

The man looks at me like I'm not making sense to him, either. He points at me and yells. Then hundreds of other men in togas swarm around me!

I run down the opposite street fast, desperate to find a way back home. I turn a corner and find myself in an Italian piazza, a wide open square in the middle of Rome. People stroll by, performers sing their best songs, and pigeons flock everywhere.

I exhale, able to stop for a moment to catch my breath, hoping the men in togas aren't following me . . . and that's when the piazza turns into a giant serving of ultra-cheesy lasagna! I sink into the gooey, saucy lasagna. Cheese wraps around my legs. It's like quicksand.

Just as the lasagna is about to pull me into its CHEESY LAIR OF DOOM permanently, my alarm goes off, waking me up. It's time to go to school.

Whew! Glad it was just a dream, but it proves to me how nervous I am about this move. Worse, I didn't dream about inventing anything.

I get ready, and then hurry off to school. My mind is pretty full, between worrying about the move to Italy and trying to come up with an idea for Sure Things, Inc.'s "last hurrah" invention.

I slip into my seat in math class.

At the very least I got my homework done, for once. That was one good thing that happened when I was trying to come up with a new invention at the office yesterday.

When Mr. Kronod, my math teacher, says, "Please pass your homework to the front of the room," I feel almost relieved. I open my backpack and reach in.

Come on, where are you? I think as I dig past last week's science test and my agenda. I reach the end of the stack of papers in my backpack. I thumb through it all again. No homework.

This is impossible. I *know* that I put it into my backpack at the office yesterday. I *know* I didn't take it out. So where is it?

One by one, I take everything out of my backpack and line it up on my desk. Out comes an old dog collar I made for Philo when he was a puppy, a half-empty bag of potato chips, three batteries, and a rainbow-colored wig—don't ask!

Okay, so I have got to clean out my backpack more often. But that doesn't matter right now.

I stare into the now-empty backpack. No math homework.

"Is there a problem, Mr. Sure?" Mr. Kronod asks, watching this all unfold.

He is the only teacher I have who calls students by their last names.

Is there a problem, Mr. Sure?

Can you round that off to three decimal places, Ms. Jenkins?

Did your parent or guardian sign the permission slip, Ms. Brown?

"Um, I'm just looking for my homework, Mr. Kronod," I say.

I search my jacket pocket, the floor under my desk, and my lunchbox. But no luck.

My math homework has gone MISSING.

I start to reload all the junk back into my pack when Mr. Kronod walks over to my desk.

"May I have your math homework, Mr. Sure?" he asks.

"Um," I say quietly. "I can't seem to find it." I gulp. "But I did it. Yes, sir, I absolutely did it. In fact I had it all completed yesterday. But I guess I left it home."

"You're a creative young man, Mr. Sure," says Mr. Kronod. "Certainly you can come up with a better excuse than that."

"But it's true!" I insist.

Mr. Kronod makes his way back to his desk.

"William Sure, unprepared," he says, marking it in his book.

I think for *just a second* about telling him that nobody ever calls me William. And that Billy is just fine. Half the time I forget my real name is William anyway. I mean, it could have been BILLYBADOODLE, right? He doesn't know that. But I think better of it and remain silent.

The end of math class doesn't come soon enough. When it finally does, I'm so flustered that I rush out into the hall, and *CRaaaaSH!!!!* right into poor Clayton Harris! Books, papers, and lunchboxes go flying.

"Billy!" Clayton says happily, showing no sign of being the least bit bothered by the fact that I just crashed into him and knocked his stuff all over the floor.

"I'm so sorry, Clayton," I reply, bending down to help him pick up everything. "I didn't see you."

When the last scrap of paper has been picked up, Clayton starts to tell me about his latest invention. I do have to get to class, but after blowing him off yesterday, not to mention crashing into him, I kind of have to listen.

"Remember the HOVER BACKPACK?" Clayton asks.

"Of course," I say.

Not too long ago Clayton showed me a backpack that he was working on. It was supposed to hover so you wouldn't have to carry heavy textbooks everywhere. "I think it's a great idea. How's it going?"

"Well, I've got the hover feature down pretty well," Clayton says. "Watch."

He picks up his backpack and presses a small button on the side. Immediately, it starts floating in midair! Then Clayton walks down the hall. The backpack follows him, hovering at arm's length.

"That's really cool!" I say. "I think kids will love it!"

"Thanks," he says. "But there's one feature I'm still having trouble with. Remember the FINDER FEATURE I tried to build in?"

"Oh yeah," I reply, recalling this from the first time Clayton showed me his invention. The finder feature finds anything that's been lost inside the Hover Backpack. "I think kids will love that, too, especially because they won't have to rummage around for everything they want to find anymore."

"Exactly," Clayton says. "But I still can't get it to work right. Here, watch." He raises his voice slightly, staring at the Hover Backpack. "Science book!"

WHOOOOOOSH!

Instantly, a large textbook comes shooting out of the backpack and goes soaring up toward the ceiling, followed by all the papers we just picked up off the floor and about half a dozen pens.

"Cool!" I tell him. Sure, he probably didn't mean for other items to come out of his backpack at the same time, but his science book did come flying out.

"I'm sure you'll fix the bugs!" I say to be encouraging.

 As soon as I say the word "bugs," I hear a lot of buzzing. *Bzzz. Bzzz. Bzzzz.* What is going on?

Suddenly, a few bugs—three flies, two bees, and six mosquitoes—come flying out of Clayton's backpack!

"How did those get in there?" Clayton wonders aloud.

Just as I think the bees are about to wreak

havoc on Fillmore Middle School, they ZOOM toward the window and disappear!

Hmm, I think, feeling a lot like Manny. I could have really used this feature when looking for my math homework earlier.

"My math homework!" I shout. "This is it!"

Clayton looks at me like I've gone crazy, and maybe I have a little. I always get kinda crazy when a new invention idea pops up. Crazy excited, that is!

"You know, Clayton, this might be too big for a backpack," I say, trying to sound a little calmer. "This finder feature should be its own invention."

"What do you mean, Billy?" Clayton asks.

"Imagine an invention that finds not just what's in your backpack, but anything you're looking for, and makes it come to you automatically!" I say.

Clayton's expression goes from concerned to worried. Not exactly the reaction I was hoping for.

"Gee, Billy, that sounds like a PRETTY

BIG PROJECT. I don't know if I can come up with that all by myself."

"Well, would you be interested in teaming up with Sure Things, Inc.?" I ask. "This sounds like the *perfect* Next Big Thing."

Clayton's face brightens. His eyes open wide.

"Really?" he asks. "You'd really want to make this product?"

I nod.

"Wooo-hooo!" Clayton whoops, as if he's just scored the final points to win the big game for his team.

As Clayton jumps around doing a happy dance, I smile, remembering that he was shy when he first joined the inventors club. I'm glad he feels comfortable around us.

"That would be awesome, Billy!" Clayton says.

"Great! Meet me at World Headquarters after school today," I say.

As I head off to my next class, I start to get excited. This really could be the invention

I've been wanting for Sure Things, Inc.'s last hurrah.

And then I get kinda sad again, thinking that there actually has to be a last hurrah at all.

Chapter Five

It's Locating! . . . Or Not

I RUSH HOME FROM SCHOOL, GRAB PHILO, AND START to head out to the office when I pass Emily. She's sitting at the couch, legs up, perusing the *Italian Words for English Speakers* dictionary.

"Have a good day *addormentato* at the office, Billy," she says.

"Thanks," I reply. "I think."

"It means 'inventing,'" Emily says.

"Actually, unless you are planning on taking a nap, Emily used the wrong word," Dad calls out from the next room where he is busy packing. "She just wished you a good day asleep!"

"Whatever!" Emily says.

A short while later Philo and I arrive at World Headquarters of Sure Things, Inc. Manny is there as usual.

"So, I invited Clayton Harris to come by this afternoon. He's been working on an invention I think you should see," I say.

"How's he doing with the inventors club, anyway?" Manny asks.

"Really great," I say. "I'm happy for him."

"And how about you?" Manny asks. "Are you doing okay with all this Italy stuff?"

Hmm. I realize now that's the first time anyone's asked how I'm doing with this. And I don't know. I'm upset? Nervous? In denial?

But before I can answer, there's a KNOCK on the door.

"Come on in!" I shout.

The door swings open and in walks Clayton, followed by the Hover Backpack, which floats along behind him. As he steps into the office, his eyes open wide and a big smile spreads across his face. He's been here before, but that was for my birthday. Everything was decorated and neatly put away then. Now Clayton gets to experience the office in all of its messy glory!

To Clayton, coming here is like going to the world's best amusement park.

"This place is so awesome!" Clayton says, looking all around. "You've got-a foosball table! And a pizza machine! And look at that *workbench!*"

Philo hops out of his doggy bed and trots over. He sniffs Clayton's shoes.

"He doesn't bite, does he?" Clayton asks nervously.

"Not unless you've invented something that turns you into a giant bowl of sausages!" Manny jokes.

Clayton laughs and scratches Philo's head. Then Philo returns to his bed and curls up for his afternoon nap.

"So this is where the magic happens?" Clayton says. "Where the All Ball was invented? Not to mention the REALLY GREAT HOVERCRAFT. Wow!"

And then I start to get nostalgic, thinking about all the fun and wacky times Manny and I have had here, all the cool inventions that came out of this little garage, and how all of that is about to come to an end.

Why does Tali DeCiso have to live in Italy, of all places?

"Nice backpack, Clayton," Manny says, snapping me back to the present. "How does the hover mechanism work?"

"Interestingly enough, I combined a few secrets ingredients with year-old peanut butter, mint toothpaste, and a little of the grease from the floor of my dad's garage," Clayton explains. "When I applied it to the backpack at just the right moment, it switched on the anti-gravity factor."

"Interesting," Manny replies. Then he turns to me. "You know, Billy, I thought it might be fun to go back to the first invention idea we ever had," he says. "Remember the day you told me about the CANDY TOOTHBRUSH?"

Wow! I haven't thought about the Candy Toothbrush for a long time.

I fill Clayton in on the details. "When I was little I *really* hated brushing my teeth, so I came up with an idea to invent a toothbrush that made any toothpaste taste like candy. I never got to work on it, though."

"Well, what about that one?" Manny asks. "The first invention idea as a last hurrah—the marketing kind of writes itself!"

"Actually, Clayton here has come up with a great idea that just needs some tweaking," I explain. "That's why I asked him to come here."

Manny looks over at the Hover Backpack.

"This is Clayton's Hover Backpack," I explain. "Not only does it hover, but it has a built-in finder feature to help you find whatever you are looking for without having to dig through everything inside."

Manny eyes it closely and then sighs.

"Well, we sold the rights to our hovercraft to the Really Great Movies studio," he explains. "So I don't think Sure Things, Inc. can release any product that hovers. I think we'd be on shaky legal ground with that one."

Clayton's expression changes immediately. Oh no. I hope I didn't tell him to come here just to leave disappointed.

"I do, however, think you might be onto something with the finder feature, Clayton," says Manny.

Clayton's whole face brightens up.

"What if we focus on that and expand it a bit?" Manny suggests. "If we can design it right, this invention should be able to find anything, anywhere, and make it come to you automatically."

"No more lost homework," I say, thinking about the possibilities.

"Or lost gummy bears," Clayton adds.

The possibilities are ENDLESS!

"Do you think we could do that, Billy?" Clayton asks. He seems a little nervous, like he's not quite sure.

"Hey, with you and me working together, why not?" I say.

The big smile returns to Clayton's face.

"I even have a name for it," says Manny.

Of course he does!

"The EVERYTHING LOCATOR!" Manny announces proudly. "Simple, easy to remember, and right to the point."

"I like it!" says Clayton. "It's a great name!"

"Manny is terrific at marketing," I say. "He'll come up with the name, the marketing plan, the sales strategy. Now, of course, all we have to do is make it perfect."

"So sometimes you guys come up with names for inventions before they're even finished?" Clayton asks.

"Are you kidding?" I say. "There have been times when Manny has come up with a whole marketing plan before I even have a working prototype!"

All three of us laugh. I think bringing Clayton into Sure Things, Inc. is going to be fun. At the same time, though, it's another reminder of how everything is about to change.

But I know what I need now. Nothing makes

me feel better faster than working on a new invention. So . . .

"Let's get busy, Clayton!" I say, leading him over to my workbench. I pull over a second stool so we can sit and work side by side.

"All right!" Clayton shouts. "HOW DO WE START?"

"Well, let's see if we can pull the finder mechanism out of the backpack," I say. "Then we can break it down and see how to expand it to find anything, anywhere, and make it come to us."

"Okay then," says Clayton, rubbing his hands together.

"If this works like we hope, it'll have so many applications," Manny says. "Just think—no more lost dogs and cats. This could be huge!"

Clayton looks over his shoulder at Manny, who is filling out a marketing plan for the Everything Locator, and then back at me.

"Manny really does plan everything before the invention even exists," he says.

I smile. "WELCOME TO SURE THINGS, INC."

Clayton works steadily, with me making suggestions as we go. About an hour later we have a working prototype. Well, a prototype. We'll find out in a minute whether it works.

"I set it up so that this device can plug into the headphone port of a smartphone," Clayton explains.

He holds up a long thin plastic box with a single wire coming out of it.

I like the way he thinks. Making an invention more accessible! Now let's see if it works.

Clayton plugs the device into his phone.

"What should I ask for, Billy?" he asks.

"How about something you already know is in this room?" I suggest.

"Hmm . . ." Clayton thinks, rubbing his chin exactly the way Manny does when he's trying to solve a problem.

"I got it," I say. I take the device and walk over to Clayton's lunchbox. I know that Clayton always has gummy bears in his lunchbox.

I hold the device up to my mouth.

"Gummy bears," I say. Nothing happens. "Gummy bears," I repeat.

Still nothing.

"Maybe you need to be closer, Billy," says Clayton.

I hold the device right above the lunchbox.

"Gummy bears," I say again. But again nothing happens.

I open the lunchbox and say it again. Still nothing.

I can see Clayton's face drooping with disappointment. To me, failures, trial and error, and constant tweaking are all part of the inventing process. But Clayton is new at this and I can see it has really gotten him down.

I lower the locator into the open lunchbox. It's so close that it's practically touching the gummy bears.

"GUMMY BEARS," I say, one more time.

Finally the device lights up and starts saying, "I have found the gummy bears" in a robotic voice.

Clayton perks up a bit.

"Okay, so we know now that it works," I say, trying to sound as cheery as possible. "What we need to do is expand the range of this invention. It's got to find everything, everywhere, like something called the Everything Locator should."

"Yes!" says Clayton. He opens up the device again and gets back to work.

A short while later we try it again.

"Red pen," I say. The device lights up. "I have found the red pen," says the robotic voice.

Something starts moving on my desk, then comes flying across the room, headed right for the Everything Locator.

"It's working!" Clayton shouts with glee.

And that's when we see what is actually flying across the room.

"That's not a pen, it's a *pin!*" I shout.

Fortunately, it's a safety pin, which happens to be closed. I snatch the pin out of midair.

"I think you need to tweak the device's hearing unit," Manny says. "Under the wrong circumstances, this could get really dangerous."

"Yes," says Clayton. "Tweaking. More tweaking."

"I think we should call it quits for the day," I say. "It's getting late. But great work today, Clayton. Really great. Can you come back tomorrow?"

"You bet, Billy!" he says.

When I pull up to my back door a little while later, I hear someone calling to me from Dad's studio (also known as the old garden shed).

"Can you come in here for a moment, Billy?" Dad asks.

Is this something about the move?

I take a deep breath, and Philo and I walk into Dad's studio.

Chapter Six

Billy Sure, Kid Painter?

DAD'S STUDIO IS PRETTY COOL. IT'S GOT THIS KIND of hip, dark lighting, and lots of sketches that will eventually become paintings. It just *feels* like my Dad's space. I wonder if he'll have a similar studio in Italy.

Tacked to the wall I see sketches of Philo's ear, Philo's toenail, Philo's nose . . . well, you get the idea. I also see the early sketches of paintings that Dad did about his favorite kitchen concoctions.

I pause at the sketch of pineapple-artichoke lasagna. I remember when Dad made that, though I've tried hard to forget. I also see a sketch of a string-bean chocolate-pudding omelet—one of Dad's Sunday morning "specials." And there's a sketch of a lobster and cheesecake wrap with a ketchup drizzle.

My brain seems to have forgotten that one, although as I look at the picture, my stomach remembers with a sick feeling.

Dad sits at his easel. His palette of paints—every color of the rainbow—sits beside him. His brushes are lined up neatly. On his art table, next to his easel, Dad has a line of shoes. Oh yeah, that's another thing—no shoes can be worn in the studio. I take my shoes off and wipe down Philo's paws.

"How's the painting going, Dad?" I ask, wondering why he called me in here in the first place.

"GREAT! GREAT!" he says, almost *too* enthusiastically. "I just started working on a new project that I think will be *perfect* for my Italian portfolio. It's a series of paintings of the bottoms of shoes—everything from work

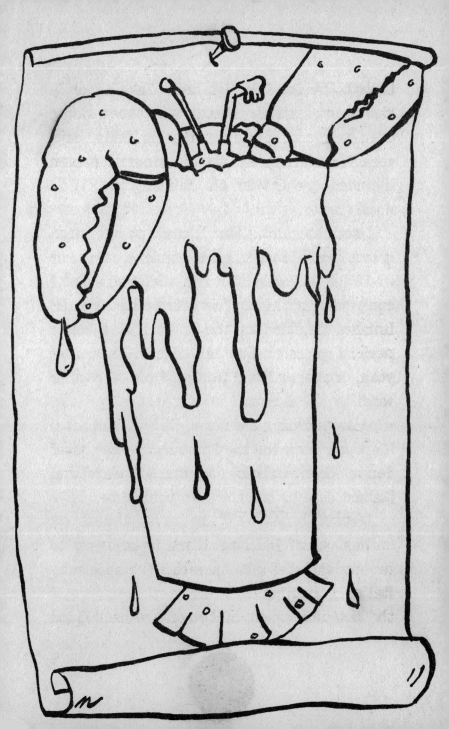

boots to sneakers to high heels. Take a look."

I look at all the sketches of shoes. Some even have gum splotches on them. Dad always goes for realism in his paintings. He even included boogers in his painting of Philo's nose.

I see the canvas Dad is working on. I find it pretty ironic that Dad is painting shoes but won't let you wear them in the studio, but I don't say anything. The canvas has a half-finished painting of the bottom of a roller skate. I guess that's kind of cool—the roller skate looks really different from a regular shoe!

"Can you do me a favor, Billy?" Dad asks. "Can you show me the bottoms of *your* shoes? You've been walking around all day, and I'd just *love* to see the dirt your shoes have collected!"

Wait, what? Did he call me in here just to see my shoes? I take them off the shoe rack and hold them up.

"Wow—that speck of dirt on the heel! Good

stuff, Billy, good stuff!" Dad says cheerfully.

"It's cool how you can get inspired by stuff most people wouldn't pay attention to otherwise," I say.

Then Dad gets an idea.

"Would *you* like try painting something, Billy?" he asks.

This really catches me by SURPRISE. I mean, I've never even thought about trying to paint outside of art class. I guess I'm just worried that my artistic talent is about as good as my singing talent—which is to say, pretty bad!

"Here's a fun thing about art," Dad says, almost like he can read my brain. "It doesn't matter if everyone else likes your painting or even if they think it's weird. As long as *you* like it, that's good enough. Remember, there are people out there who think the *Mona Lisa* is terrible!"

Hmm. I never thought of it that way—painting for *you*, and not other people. That's definitely not how it works with inventing.

I do have to say, though, this makes perfect sense coming from Dad, considering the kinds of paintings he does. I suddenly feel REALLY PROUD of my dad. And I suddenly decide that, you know what? It might actually be fun to paint.

"Thanks, Dad," I say, picking up a paintbrush. "Let's get this started!"

Dad quickly sets up a second easel next to his. He pulls out a fresh canvas and another palette of paints.

"So, what do you think you'd like to paint?" he asks.

I think about it for a second.

"I want to paint things that I don't want to forget when we move to Italy," I say.

Dad nods and goes back to his own painting.

I start by sketching out what I hope looks like the World Headquarters of Sure Things, Inc. Only it doesn't really look like the headquarters at all. It kinda looks lopsided and weird.

Before I start to judge myself, I remember what Dad just said.

As long as you like it, that's good enough.

I go back to work, adding colors to my sketch. Soon I have a painting of the World Headquarters—or at least the Billy Sure version of the World Headquarters, complete with aliens and elves, because I kinda think it would be cool to work with aliens and elves.

I go on to paint a picture of the outside of Fillmore Middle School and the constant mess that is my room at home. I would paint Philo, but looking around . . . I think Dad's got that covered. Also, Philo is coming to Italy with us.

"What do you think, Dad?" I ask when I'm done.

Dad puts down his brushes and walks over to my easel. He stares for a second, scratching his chin.

"I like these," he says. "They are unique. They are expressive. And mostly, THEY ARE YOU. Nobody else told you what to paint. I love that. Now, why don't you try to push your creative boundaries even further?"

"I'm not sure I know what you mean," I say.

"One great thing about painting is that it's not a photograph," Dad explains. "It doesn't have to show the real world as it would look if you took a photo."

I think I understand what Dad means, although, glancing at my paintings again, I can't imagine anyone confusing them for photographs.

"Let your imagination go," Dad continues. "Think of a place you'd like to be, even one you've never actually seen, and imagine what it might look like. That's a pretty good place to start."

Then Dad goes back to his own painting.

Hmm . . . a place I'd like to see that I've never been to . . . oh, I know! Space! Before I got into inventing, I wanted to be an astronaut. I've also always wanted to see Earth from space.

Excited and energized, I start sketching out the globe. Soon I have a picture of Earth as it might be seen from space.

It doesn't have to show the real world . . .

And then I add a finishing touch. I paint another planet right next to it—this time, a Philo planet!

"What do you think, Dad?" I say. "I guess you could say that Philo is in his own orbit!"

Dad looks over and smiles. "I love it, Billy! I love how you used your imagination. After all, that's what art is all about!"

Dad's a pretty smart guy. I think he knows how worried I am about this upcoming move and this really helped take my mind off of it for a little while. Painting also helps me feel a little closer to him. Yup, a pretty smart guy.

I show Philo the painting, but he doesn't seem to register the dog planet as him, even though I say, "That's *you*, boy!" I wish I had the CAT-DOG TRANSLATOR on me right now.

I grab my painting and head into the house. Dad is right behind me, having just finishing his painting of, um . . . my shoe. As soon as I walk through the front door, Emily comes over to me.

"What's that?" she asks, pointing at my canvas.

I flip the painting around, bracing myself for whatever mean thing my older sister is probably going to say.

"Ah, Philo *sotto il letto*," Emily says. "For you Americans, that means 'Philoworld.'"

"Actually, honey, what you said means 'Philo under the bed,'" Dad explains.

I snicker. "Well, who's to say that Emily doesn't interpret my painting as a picture of a bed with Philo under it?"

"Very funny," Emily says. "Or as we say in Italy, *molto finestra!*"

We say in Italy? So now Emily is suddenly a native Italian person?

"You just said 'VERY WINDOW,' sweetie," Dad tells her. "That doesn't make much sense."

"Well, neither does Billy's painting," Emily says, shrugging. She heads to the kitchen.

I don't let Emily's comments bother me.

"I'm going to hang this at World Headquarters tomorrow," I tell Dad. "That way, whenever Manny looks at it he'll think of me . . . and Philo, of course. Philo didn't do much inventing, but he *did* come to the office with me every day."

Philo yips in agreement.

• • •

The next day after school I bring my painting to the office. Manny and Clayton are already there when I arrive.

"What's that, Billy?" Clayton asks, pointing to the painting.

I flip it around and hold it up for them to see.

"A Philo planet!" Clayton says.

At the sound of his name, Philo barks, trots over to Clayton, and licks his face. Clayton giggles.

"I think it should go there," Manny says, pointing to a spot on the wall above Philo's doggy bed.

"Great," I say.

With Clayton's help, the painting is soon hung.

"All right," I say, stepping back and admiring my painting. I have to admit, this little exercise was a lot of fun, but the time has now come for my real work—inventing!

Clayton and I head over to my workbench and take apart the prototype we built yesterday.

"So the problem at this point is RANGE," I

remind Clayton. "We want this thing to find a missing object no matter how far away it is."

"If we increase the amplification level of the tracking sensor, that could help a lot," Clayton says.

"Which one is the tracking sensor?" I ask, staring into the open device at a jumble of wires, circuit boards, and connectors.

"This thing here," Clayton says, pointing.

"That looks like a peanut shell," I say. "What is it?"

"A peanut shell made of metal," Clayton replies. "I have found that it holds certain connectors together very well, and is just small enough to fit inside the device."

Clayton digs in. He pushes, bends, and adjusts most of the components. I pull out my boxes of parts, and he rummages through those, gathering what he needs. I help him when I can, but he seems to have this under control.

After about an hour he's ready to do a test. We plug the device into Clayton's phone.

"What should we have it find, Billy?" he asks.

I look around. I spot a red phone all the way on the other side of the room.

"How about that red phone?" I say. "That's a pretty good distance away."

Clayton nods. Then he leans over to the device and says, "Red phone."

Ding! Ding! Ding! The device starts beeping and flashing. I hear a rattling from across the room.

"It's working!" I say.

Suddenly, one of Philo's dog bones comes flying toward us! It lands next to the device. Then another bone comes flying in our direction . . . only this one is still in Philo's mouth!

Eyes wide, ears flapping behind him, Philo comes soaring through the air, being propelled forward by the bone in his mouth. Thankfully, I catch him before he crashes into the workbench, and place him back down on the floor.

"Looks like the device still has a hearing problem," I say. "Red *phone*, not dog bone. Back to work."

Once again we open up the device and get busy. After a few more trials Clayton and I still haven't come very far.

"This is the point where I start to wonder if maybe I should give up," I say under my breath.

"Who said anything about GIVING UP?" Manny asks, speaking up for the first time since we began tweaking the device. Manny never interferes with the actual creative inventing process, but he's always there to offer encouragement—like he just did. Reason #399 why I'm going to miss seeing Manny every day once I go to Italy.

"What do we do now, Billy?" Clayton asks.

Manny and I look at each other. We both know what needs to happoen next. "Sleep-invent!" we say in unison.

"Can you do that, Billy?" Clayton asks hopefully.

"I've done it lots of times," I say. And I have. Usually when I'm in the middle of a project or close to being done with it, I sleep-invent. While I'm sleeping, I draft up some blueprints that solve whatever problems I've been having with my invention.

"Cool!" says Clayton. "I can't wait to see what you come up with!"

With that, we decide to wrap things up for today. Clayton leaves and I walk over to Manny's desk. It's time for me to tell Manny something I've been mulling over for a while.

"You know, Manny," I say, feeling kinda nervous. "I think that once I'm gone, Clayton might be able to help you. I mean, having someone here in the office has always been good for us. Even though I'll be video-chatting in, he could be my hands, so to speak."

To my surprise, Manny shrugs.

"I like Clayton," he says. "But we'll have to see, Billy. Let's not make any decisions right now."

I nod, then head for home.

When I walk through the front door, I see all the paintings I made with Dad lined up in the hallway, waiting to be wrapped and shipped to Italy.

Emily walks up and down the hall, looking at the paintings as if our hallway has become an ART GALLERY OPENING. She pauses and looks at each one, tilting her head slightly to the side, stepping back for a better view.

Here it comes, some snarky comment, as if she were an art critic about to write a one-star review for a fancy art magazine.

"You know, Billy," Emily says after a few more moments of looking, tilting, and stepping around. "You are actually a pretty *buono scoiattolo*."

"Thanks," I say. "I think."

Dad speaks up from the next room where he is packing. "I know you are trying to tell Billy that he's a pretty good painter, Em, but you actually called him 'a good squirrel.'"

"I meant to say that!" Emily says, then she heads up to her room.

I follow her upstairs and go to my room where I stare at a bunch of empty boxes. In the morning, the move to Italy will be ten days away, and I still haven't packed a single thing.

I just can't bring myself to start. How do you start packing all your stuff to move to another country?! If only I could SLEEP-PACK....

Sleep! That reminds me. I have to sleep-invent the solutions to the problems we've been having with the Everything Locator tonight. Just what I need—more pressure!

Chapter Seven

Locate Everything

I WAKE UP THE NEXT MORNING FEELING ENERGIZED, and not just because it's a Saturday. Did my sleep-inventing work like I'd hoped?

I rush to my desk and there they are—fully rendered blueprints for the Everything Locator! I look through the plans, and as usual with my sleep-inventing, they make perfect sense.

It's funny. When I invented the All Ball, I didn't know about sleep-inventing. See, I usually can recognize my own handwriting, but as it turns out, when I sleep-invent, I use my *left* hand even though I'm right-handed, and the handwriting from my left hand looks a lot different! So for a while there I wondered if maybe someone else snuck in and invented the All Ball for me. Thankfully, I found out it was all me. My left handwriting is a bit messier, but that's okay. The point is, it helps me sleep-invent and I now have blueprints, so I'm a pretty happy kid.

I grab my phone and text Manny and Clayton. We agree to meet at the office this afternoon—which gives me plenty of time to build a rough prototype for when we're there.

Before that happens, though, I head downstairs for some breakfast. As I make my way down, I notice boxes on every step.

Our house is starting to look more like a warehouse than a home! Boxes line every wall. Plastic bubble wrap sits in huge heaps right in the middle of the living room. Honestly? I don't want to look at this anymore. It makes me feel kind of QUEASY.

I join the rest of my family at the kitchen

table, which is the only place left without boxes everywhere.

"Eggplant pancakes with banana-chili syrup," Dad announces as I take my seat. He plops a stack of purple pancakes onto my plate.

We all munch on our pancakes for a little while in silence. It's weird. Usually we're a talkative bunch. I think we're all focused on the impending move.

"I have to go to the office later," I say, breaking the silence.

"You still have all your packing to do, honey," says Mom.

"I know." I shove another bite of purple pancake into my mouth. "I'll get it done. But I need to nail down this final invention Manny and I have been working on."

"No rest for the *assonnato*," Emily mutters.

"No rest for the sleepy?" Dad asks.

"No, 'weary,'" Emily whines in reply. "No rest for the weary!"

I have to admit that Emily's latest thing is starting to get, I don't know, just a *little* bit annoying. I mean, I don't mind if she wants to speak Italian, but she has no idea what any of the words mean!

After breakfast I rush back up to my room and shove aside papers, wires, and empty tin cans (don't ask), knocking them off my home workbench. Here at home is where my inventing first started. Long before the All Ball and Sure Things, Inc., I taught myself how to invent right here in this room.

I prop up the blueprints on my desk and read them, compiling a list of all the parts I'll need to build a working prototype of the Everything Locator.

Let's see . . . hmm . . . it looks like one of the main things I'll need is a ton of paper clips— pretty much every paper clip in the house to make sure it's right.

I start pulling open every drawer in my room. I empty a dish of paper clips into a plastic bag, making sure I fish out a couple of thumb tacks, the tops of five old pens, and a small piece of burrito that's probably . . . well, older than I'd like to admit.

When I'm pretty sure that I've gotten every paper clip in my room, I move on to Emily's room.

"What do you want?" she asks, when I appear at her door holding my bag of paper clips.

"What, no Italian?" I ask.

"I can say it in any language you like, but it all means the same thing." Emily furrows her brow at me. "WHAT. DO. YOU. WANT!"

"Paper clips," I reply.

"Looks like you have a couple . . . hundred!" she says, pointing at the plastic bag, which is starting to stretch from the weight of all those clips.

"I need a ton," I say. "Well, a lot, is what I mean."

Emily sighs her "Oh, the things I have to put up with" sigh, slides her chair away from her desk, and gestures for me to come on in.

"I'm not getting up," she says, "but feel free to look yourself."

 I pull open each drawer in Emily's desk, scooping any stray paper clips into my bag. The bag gets heavier and heavier until I worry that it might break. And then I'm done.

"Thanks," I say, heading out of Emily's room.

Just before I leave the room, Emily says, "Billy, can I borrow a paper clip?"

I sigh my "Oh, the things I have to put up with" sigh and continue on my way.

Mom's home office is next. My mom is so super organized that this should be a piece of cake. I fully expect to find boxes with printed labels saying SMALL PAPER CLIPS, MEDIUM PAPER CLIPS, RED PAPER CLIPS, and so on.

But when I walk into her office, I'm stunned. The whole office is packed up and ready to be shipped to Italy!! Big boxes line the room from floor to ceiling. Just as I turn to leave, I spot a renegade paper clip on the floor. I pick it up, toss it into my bag, and head back to my workbench. I guess finding one is better than nothing?

About an hour later, I'm ready. I've made all the adjustments indicated in my sleep-invented blueprints, and now it's time for a test.

I head outside and plug the prototype into my phone.

Okay, HERE GOES. I might as well start by searching for the thing that started this whole idea—my math homework!!!

I switch on the device.

"Math homework," I say as clearly as I

possibly can. "The math homework that I lost!"

Beep! Beep! Beep! The Everything Locator lights up! I start to get excited. Good old sleep-inventing. Works every time.

But then a few seconds pass and nothing happens. No math homework comes flying into my hands.

What's going on here? Could these blueprints be faulty? What do I do now?

Just as I'm thinking all of this and preparing for the WORST CASE scenario, the prototype starts beeping. I look up and see Philo walking toward me. Only he's walking in a really strange way. It's almost like he's being pulled toward me by some kind of . . . of . . . DOG MAGNET. Like he's not really moving under his own power.

"You okay, bud?" I ask. "What's going on?" A few seconds later Philo reaches where I'm standing and sticks to me like glue. I go to pick him up, but I can't move him. It's like he's magnetically stuck to my leg!

I look up and see what I can only describe

as a BLIZZARD OF STUFF flying right at me through the open front window of our house. Stacks of blueprints speed through the air. The papers hit me and also stick—at the same time some toy dragons stick to my shoe!

A deck of cards emerges from the tsunami of stuff flying from the house. The whole deck spreads out, each one of the fifty-two cards, and covers about half my body.

But that's not all. A rubber chicken lands on my head, and no matter how hard I pull, I can't get it off. A piece of pizza with some disgusting green stuff on it slams into my leg and sticks, right next to where Philo is stuck.

Philo licks his lips.

"No, boy! Don't eat that!"

I pull Philo away just in time.

And the stuff just keeps on coming. And sticking to me. This started out weird, then maybe a little funny, but now . . . now I'm plain old stuck in this junk!

And then something I really *did* lose

comes flying at me. No, not the elusive math homework, but a prototype of the CAT-DOG TRANSLATOR. Okay, I know I've said in the past that I hid it away for safekeeping, and that was true . . . I just wasn't sure *where* I hid it. I wasn't sure if I'd ever see it again. And I'm not so sure I'm happy to see it now. It—you guessed it—sticks right to me.

But stuff keeps coming! Papers and empty boxes and small framed pictures and toys and hats and everything you can think of. I'm getting buried, standing here on the lawn in front of my house!

And then I have a thought.

I need to *turn OFF the Everything Locator*!

That should be easy, all I need is to unplug it from my phone . . . but, oh no. Where *is* my phone? I had put it down and now it's nowhere to be seen. It must be covered in the other lost stuff! I can't find it and I can't call anyone for help.

"Philo, how are we ever going to dig our way out of this?" I ask, glancing down. He is still stuck to my leg. I really wish Philo could answer me, maybe even offer some wise advice.

Wait a minute! Maybe he can!

I move the Cat-Dog Translator down toward Philo and turn it on.

"GIVE ME AN IDEA, BOY!"

Thankfully, it works just like it's supposed to.

"We need to *smell* our way out!" Philo barks into the translator.

Then Philo starts smelling things in the pile. "Nope—not a door," he says while sniffing the rubber chicken.

"Nope—not a window," he says while sniffing a set of house keys.

"Nope—not a door," he repeats, sniffing at some of my dirty laundry. "I like the way your socks smell, Billy!"

I quickly realize that Philo is not going to be much help in solving this problem. I turn off the Cat-Dog Translator.

I'm going to have to dig my way out!

Thankfully, there's a small plastic shovel near me. I think I used to take it to the beach when I was a little kid. I take it and prod at a few things, but it doesn't really help. I decide to dig my way out the good ol' fashioned way—with my hands!

I start pulling off stuff. But every time I remove something, something else—an egg beater, a lamp, a set of plastic cups, cardboard packing boxes, a tortilla comes flying at me and sticks to the pile like glue.

There's just too much stuff.

It's EVERYWHERE!

I'm starting to lose sight of the house—and more stuff just keeps on coming!

What am I going to do?!?!

Chapter Eight

The "Something" Locator?

JUST WHEN I THINK I'M GOING TO BE STUCK IN THIS pile of junk forever, I hear a voice.

"Billy!"

Oh no. I've read about people who are in impossible situations, like lost in deserts, and start seeing mirages of water. Is this voice a MIRAGE?! Am I doomed?!

"Billy!" the voice calls again.

It sounds far away. At this point I can't see anything. Too much stuff blocks my view. I turn my head to the left and get a face full of bubble wrap. I turn to the right and my view is blocked by a lamp, a framed picture, and a carton of milk.

"Billy!"

Okay, either that voice is real, or I'm really starting to let this trapped thing get the best of me!

"Billy, it's Manny!"

Manny? Now I perk up.

"Manny! I'm stuck in the middle of this pile of stuff!" I shout, hoping it really is him.

"I'm working on it!" Manny yells back.

I hear rustling. Yup, this is real—my best friend is definitely here.

I start shoving stuff aside from the center of the pile as Manny does the same from the outside. *Clunk. clunk. clunk.* The stuff keeps plopping to the floor. In a few minutes a hand breaks through the wall of stuff.

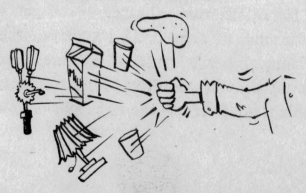

"Hold on, boy," I tell Philo, and tuck him under my arm. I grab Manny's hand with my free arm and we get pulled forward.

And then we're out! I have never felt freer in my life. This feels even better than the last day of school before summer vacation.

I place Philo on the ground safely, and then fall down to the grass, exhausted. I see that in his other hand Manny is holding my phone.

"You might want this," he says, pulling the locator device out of my phone. Instantly, all the stuff in the huge pile I've just escaped falls onto the front lawn.

All except for the Cat-Dog Translator, which Philo has firmly in his mouth.

"Thanks for rescuing me, Manny," I say. "How did you know I was stuck?"

"When it takes you over an hour to bike to the office from your house, and you stop answering calls and texts, I know something is wrong," Manny explains. "I figured I'd ride over and make sure everything was okay. I definitely did *not* expect to see, well . . . *that*."

"Yeah, me neither," I say.

"What happened?" Manny asks.

"I successfully sleep-invented the blueprints for the Everything Locator," I say. "It showed me exactly where Clayton and I went wrong with the prototype we developed in the office. It also showed me exactly how to fix it. I figured that I would whip up a quick prototype at home so I could bring it when I joined you guys at the office later, and we could maybe celebrate with some pizza."

"So far, so good," says Manny.

"Yeah, until I tested it," I say. "I brought it out here, plugged it into my phone, and asked it find my math homework. And, well, that's when everything started flying toward me and stuck to me as if I were a giant magnet."

"Hmm," says Manny.

"Yeah—on the bright side, it found a lot of stuff I'd lost," I say.

At this, Philo drops the translator onto the ground and the device switches on. *Ding!*

The Cat-Dog Translator does its thing as Philo barks.

"The door!" Philo says, wagging his tail and licking Manny's face. "Manny human found the door. My Billy human and I are saved!"

Manny and I crack up. Dogs are pretty funny that way! Then I pick up the translator and switch it off. As we learned when we first invented the thing, dogs don't really have a filter. It's not always the best idea to know everything your dog is saying. For example, I really don't need Philo to start telling Manny that I drooled the shape of Tennessee on my pillow last night.

"We better clean up this mess," Manny says, staring at the pretty sizable pile of junk.

"I'll deal with it later," I say. "Let's just stick everything in the garage for now."

Manny helps me haul all the junk from the house into the garage. We use a red wagon that came along in the pile to get everything there safely in only a few trips.

"I still can't figure out why this all went

so wrong," I say, carrying a rice cooker in one hand and a hair dryer in the other. "The blueprints looked pretty good to me."

"Where are they?" Manny asks.

"I don't see them here, so they must still be up in my room," I say.

"Come on," says Manny. "Let's go take a look."

A few moments later I unroll the blueprints. I do a double check just in case—yup, I followed these instructions exactly. I pass them to Manny to look over. Then he opens up the prototype I built. Paper clips spill out all over the floor.

"How many paper clips did you use?" he asks.

"Well, the blueprints weren't exactly specific," I explain. "They just said to use 'a ton' of paper clips. So I did."

Manny looks closely at the blueprints and squints.

"Um, actually, Billy, I think what you wrote here is 'ten' paper clips, not a 'ton' of paper clips," he says.

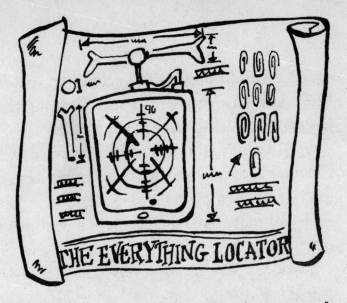

THE EVERYTHING LOCATOR

"What?!" I lean in closely. Sure enough, now, with Manny pointing it out to me, I can see that I wrote "TEN paper clips." Leave it to Manny to read my left-handed handwriting better than I can! Reason #1029 I'm glad he's my business partner.

I slap my forehead in disbelief and shake my head. "Well, that explains a lot, doesn't it?"

I kneel down and pick up all the paper clips off the floor, counting out ten and slipping those into my pocket.

Manny glances at his phone. "Come on," he says. "Let's go meet Clayton at the office."

With Philo in tow, Manny and I hop on our bikes and ride over to World Headquarters. Clayton is waiting there when we arrive.

I fill Clayton in on what happened with the prototype. Manny sits at his computer and starts scanning through sales figures. It may be a Saturday, but for Manny, it's business as usual.

"Well, it did locate everything," Clayton points out. "Isn't that what something called the Everything Locator should do?"

"No," Manny replies immediately.

I'm stunned at first by Manny's answer. Then I look over at him. He has an expression on his face that I know all too well. As he often does, Manny has thought of something that nobody else has.

"No?" Clayton repeats, sounding baffled. "An Everything Locator *shouldn't* be able to locate everything?"

"No," Manny says again.

Now Clayton and I are both confused. Manny turns toward us and continues.

"The device we invent should locate everything, or, more accurately, *anything* a person is
looking for. But maybe it shouldn't return that
item to the person. I feel like we'll run into a
lot of clogged airways with that."

I'm not sure I understand where Manny is
going with this. I always thought the thing
that would make this invention popular was
that all you had to do was say the name of a
lost item, and bingo!—it's right there in your
hands.

"There are lots of situations, as Billy just
found out, where having a lost item come flying at you may not be the best idea," Manny
goes on. "What if the item is large and acci-
dentally hits someone during its flight to you
from who knows where? It could hurt someone, or crash through a window, or arrive
smashed to pieces it if runs into something
on the way . . . maybe we've been going about
this wrong."

This is starting to make sense.

"Maybe, instead of the Everything Locator—

and yes, Clayton, I still like that name—the device could find what you are looking for, and give you detailed directions on how to get to wherever the missing item is. There are phone apps that already exist for finding your lost phone, but this would find, well, *everything*. Then you could go and get it."

"We can incorporate a micro device that gives directions," Clayton says. "There should be enough room inside to work that in."

"Especially if you only use *ten* paper clips!" Manny says, not even bothering to turn around.

He doesn't have to. I can tell that he's smiling.

And that is reason #15 why I am going to miss working here in the office with Manny once I move to Italy. We can basically READ EACH OTHER'S MINDS.

Clayton and I get started, working with the correct amount of paper clips for the device and the micro device Clayton mentioned.

I must admit it, Clayton and I have become

a pretty good team. Sometimes when building a new invention, four hands are better than two.

A little while later we're ready for our first test. I plug the new prototype into my phone and power it up. **Ding! Ding! Ding!** It flashes and beeps.

"So far, so good," says Clayton, showing a toothy smile. "What should we ask it to find?"

My first thought, of course, is to ask it to find my missing math homework, since, you know, out of *everything* the first locator found, it didn't seem to find that! But I figure we should start off with something simple.

"How about my favorite sneakers?" I say, looking down at my flip-flops and thinking of Dad's latest paintings. "They're in my closet at home. They should be fairly easy for the device to find."

"Okay," says Clayton. He leans in close to the device and speaks. "Find Billy's favorite sneakers."

Beep! Beep! Beep!

"I think it's working!" Clayton shouts.

Just like that, the screen on my phone lights up and displays a map leading from the World Headquarters to a store called Shelley's Sneaker Spectacular!

"Well, it found sneakers, only not *your* sneakers, Billy," Clayton says, less excited now.

Billy's Favorite Sneakers

"Hmm . . . let's make a few adjustments," I say, turning back to the device.

After a few more tweaks I'm ready to try again.

"This time, let's look for my space helmet," Clayton says. "I think my mom put it up in our attic."

I hold back from asking Clayton why he has a space helmet. If he has plans to travel to Mars, he certainly hasn't told me about them. But I guess he can tell from my expression that I'm wondering about this.

"I used to want to be an astronaut when I grow up," Clayton explains. "So my mom got me a space helmet. When I told her that I changed my mind and that now I want to be an inventor, she packed the helmet away. It still would be cool for Halloween costumes, though, if we find it."

I nod, then switch on the prototype.

"Clayton's space helmet," I say into the device.

Beep! Beep! Beep!

Again, the screen blazes to life. This time it shows a large map leading from the World Headquarters of Sure Things, Inc. . . . right to the International Space Station!

"I'm sure you'll find lots of space helmets there, Clayton," I say. "Just not the one in your attic. Back to work."

After a few more adjustments, we try for a third time. I'm starting to get a little discouraged. What if our last hurrah invention is one big, giant FAILURE?

Manny, who has been quietly analyzing sales figures, speaks up.

"How about testing it with something simple and close by?" he suggests.

"How about Philo?" Clayton says.

"Okay," I say, bringing the device up to my chin. "Philo," I say clearly into it.

Beep! Beep! Beep!

The screen lights up and shows a path leading directly from my workbench to Philo's doggy bed, where he is happily curled up, snoring. *Zzzz!*

"Success!" I say. "Now let's try to find something outside the garage. Hmm, I know! My bike."

More beeping. This time, the screen shows

a path leading out the front door right to my bike!

"I think we've done it, Clayton!" I say, giving him a high five.

Just then I hear more beeping coming from my phone.

"Is there something wrong with the Everything Locator?" Clayton asks, looking worried.

I look down at the screen. Thankfully, it isn't the Everything Locator app—it's just my normal, regular phone.

"I'm getting a text," I explain.

The screen flashes and I see the contact who sent the message. Mom.

> B, you need to pack. We are moving very soon!

A feeling of dread washes over me. My mom never, ever sends demanding texts like this, but she's right—I've been procrastinating, and I don't have a whole lot of time left.

"Mom wants me to come home and start packing," I say glumly.

"You haven't started?" Manny asks.

"I'll get it done," I say. "It's just been . . . it's been hard, that's all. I gotta go. I'll see you guys later."

I start biking home. Philo trots alongside me. As I pedal, I feel kinda mixed-up. I'm thrilled that we now have a working prototype of the Everything Locator. I'm happy that Clayton was such a big help.

But I can't push off the fact any longer—ten days from today we are leaving, going thousands of miles and a GREAT BIG OCEAN away. I have to go home and pack. I try to focus on that, separate from everything else it means.

I walk through our front door and find myself up to my eyeballs in boxes. The house hardly looks like our house anymore. Most of the furniture has been wrapped up in padded blankets. The walls are bare, except for the black smudgy lines showing where the paintings used to hang.

I head up to my room, which is filled with boxes—empty boxes, but boxes nonetheless. Mom must have put them in here when I was gone.

I open every drawer in my dresser and in my desk. I fling open my closet door and sigh, looking at all the stuff I've crammed in there over the years. I can hardly see the floor, and the shelf up top is sagging from the weight of my comic books and baseball cards, which are neatly stored in boxes stacked on top of one another.

As my mind races and I think about all of the things I'm going to miss, a stack of empty boxes starts sliding toward me.

Ka-Raaaash!

And that's when the boxes tumble down, scattering around my room. And there stands Philo, who had been hiding under the boxes.

I start laughing and drop to the floor, rolling around with Philo, who barks and licks my face as we play-wrestle, just like we've done since he was a little puppy.

And I start to feel like maybe all this might not be so bad. After all, Philo will be there with me in Italy. I'll still have my pal by my side, and that should help make wherever I am feel like home. Who says we can't play-wrestle in Italy, too?

I go back to my packing with a renewed burst of energy, feeling like somehow this is going to be okay.

Chapter Nine

Field Test

THE NEXT MORNING, I REALIZE IT'S MY SECOND- to-last Sunday at home. So I decide to have a little fun. I text Clayton and Manny.

> Breakfast this morning at Waldo's World of Pancakes?

I remember the moment just after my last birthday when Mom and Dad told me that I was finally old enough to go out to a restaurant without them—as long as it is less than a ten-minute bike ride, and that I promise to have my cell phone out on the table so I'm sure to not miss their phone call.

Seemed like a pretty good deal to me—all except for the phone on the table part. The first time I met Manny for pancakes at Waldo's I spilled maple syrup all over my phone.

Have you ever seen a phone covered in maple syrup? Well, I hope you never do. It's a sticky situation. But at least it smells delicious!

My phone beeps a few seconds later. It's Manny:

> Sure, sounds good . . . Don't forget to bring a plastic bag for your phone. ☺

I can see now that I'm never going to live down the infamous maple-syrup-on-the-phone incident.

Then a text comes in from Clayton:

> Sorry, Billy. Can't. Band practice. Have to work on my sousaphone solo.

Attached to Clayton's text is a photo of him playing his sousaphone. I giggle a bit at the sight of Clayton surrounded by this huge brass instrument that wraps around and towers over him.

A few minutes later I'm biking my way toward Waldo's World of Pancakes. It takes less than ten minutes to arrive. Inside, Manny is already waiting at our favorite booth—also known as "THE TABLE CLOSEST TO THE TOPPINGS BAR," where you can pile everything from bananas to chocolate chips onto your pancakes.

"Too bad Clayton couldn't make it," Manny says as I slip into the booth. "I've been thinking a lot about how he can help us when you're away."

"Yeah, me too," I say.

Our waitress comes over.

"What can I get you boys?" she asks.

"I'll have a big stack, please," I say.

"Same for me," says Manny.

"Clayton is busy," I say, once the waitress has left with our order. "He's got his schoolwork, and he runs the inventors club, and he's in the band, too. I worry a little that he might not have as much time as he needs to devote to working with you at Sure Things, Inc. And I don't want him to feel overwhelmed, either."

"I'm not worried," Manny says.

Of course not. Manny is never worried.

"Here's how I figure it," Manny says. "The big ideas will still come from you, Billy. And from time to time you may still have to sleep-invent."

Manny continues. "I see Clayton's role as the guy who tinkers with your ideas, builds, and reworks prototypes at HQ. I'll be working beside him on the marketing and business side. And we can video-chat you in if Clayton gets stuck with the hands-on stuff."

As our conversation continues, my mood really starts to pick up. I am leaving Sure Things, Inc. in good hands, and I won't be gone completely. I can join in on the conversations at World Headquarters any time I need to—or want to, for that matter.

"This all seems to make a lot of sense, Manny," I say. "Clayton can give us as much time as works for him. And speaking of time . . . it seems to be taking an awfully long time for our pancakes to arrive, right? I wonder where they are?"

Maybe I'm just hungry, but it feels like it's been hours since the server took our order!

"Well, if we had an Everything Locator, we could find out!" Manny says, smiling.

I laugh.

"Oh, wait, I just happen to have one here!" Manny says in his cheesy marketing voice. He opens up his backpack, pulls out the prototype, and plugs it into my phone.

"Everything Locator? Where are our pancakes?" I say into the device.

Beep! Beep! Beep!

The prototype starts beeping and blinking. After a few seconds a map appears on the phone's screen. It shows a path leading right from our table to the kitchen!

"Well, that makes sense that our food is in the kitchen," Manny says. "In fact, I'd be concerned if it was hanging out outside. But it still doesn't explain what's taking so long."

I look around the restaurant. It doesn't look crowded. At least not more crowded than every other time we've come here. Then I notice something.

"Hey, look, the blinking light on the map is moving," I say, pointing at my phone's screen.

"It's coming toward us," Manny says. "Mmm. Looks like breakfast is on the way."

A few seconds later the blinking light is right next to our location.

"Our pancakes should be here now!" I say.

"Would you like me to put them on the table?" says a voice that startles us both. Our eyes have been so focused on the phone screen that we didn't even notice the fact that the waitress is standing right next to us.

"Thanks," I say, a bit embarrassed.

The waitress places an enormous stack of pancakes in front of each of us. They smell delicious.

"What's that thing?" the waitress asks, pointing at the Everything Locator. "Some kind of CRAZY NEW SMARTPHONE?"

"Have you ever lost anything?" Manny asks her.

"Are you kidding? Every day!" she replies, setting the maple syrup down next to our plates. "In fact, just this morning, after I got here, I lost my car keys. I don't know how I'm going to get home later. In fact, that's why it took me so long to bring out your pancakes. I'm really sorry about that. I was searching the whole kitchen for my keys, but no luck."

Like magic, as soon as the waitress says the words "car keys," the Everything Locator lights up! It starts beeping and, lo and behold, a new map appears on the screen! A path pops up leading from our table back into the kitchen. A window within the screen shows a close-up map indicating the keys' exact location.

"I think you'll find your keys on the right front corner of the stove in the kitchen," I say, feeling proud of how specific the Everything Locator has become.

The waitress looks at me like I'm a little nuts. And who can blame her? I'm here with a weird-looking contraption, and I somehow can magically tell her that I know where her lost keys are? She shrugs and returns to the kitchen.

Manny and I head to the toppings bar, where I load up my big stack with chocolate-covered peanuts, strawberry jam, and crunchy peanut butter. Then it's back to the table to cover it all with syrup. We dive right into the mountain of food in front of us.

I've hardly had a chance to swallow my first bite when the waitress comes hurrying from the kitchen. In her hand she holds a napkin.

"THAT THING IS AMAZING!" she says, pointing at the Everything Locator. She holds out the napkin, and there, sitting in the middle,

is a set of car keys covered in what looks like green goop.

"There is a pot of split pea soup cooking on the right front burner of the stove," she explains. "I made that soup when I got in this morning. Sure enough, in the bottom of the pot were my car keys. They must have fallen in as I was putting the soup together."

Manny and I look at each other and smile. This thing works better than I thought.

"I want to thank you boys," the waitress says. "Not only did you help me find my keys, but you prevented one of my lunch customers from getting a big surprise in their soup later! Can I get one of those FINDER THINGS?"

"It's called the Everything Locator," Manny says in his best marketing voice. "And we're very close to a deal that will have this device in every major store by next month."

"Well, you've got one customer, for sure," says the waitress. "Now I have to go make a new pot of soup. Thanks again!"

"Nothing like a real field test," I say when the waitress has left.

"And real-time customer satisfaction," Manny adds. "This one could be big, Billy. Just like we wanted for our last hurrah."

Ah—just like that, my mixed feelings about moving come spiraling back. Working on this invention lifted my spirits and took my mind off the move (for the most part). But now the Everything Locator works, and in only a few days I'll be leaving.

It's strange how my brain flits around sometimes. Here I am thinking about all this stuff, but what pops out of my mouth is, "And I still need to find my missing math homework!" After all, that *is* what started this whole thing. Even though I won't be in Mr. Kronod's math class much longer, I kind of want to redeem myself to him!

As I say "math homework," the Everything Locator lights up and starts beeping. A new map pops up on the screen. It shows a path leading out of the restaurant directly to a nearby park!

"I forgot this thing was on!" I say. "But this has to be a mistake. Why would my math homework be in the park?"

"Well, the Everything Locator has been right so far," Manny points out. "Let's go find out."

We both shovel the final forkfuls of topping-and-syrup-smothered pancakes into our mouths, pay, and hurry from the restaurant, eager to see what the Everything Locator has, well . . . LOCATED.

We follow the path past a line of stores,

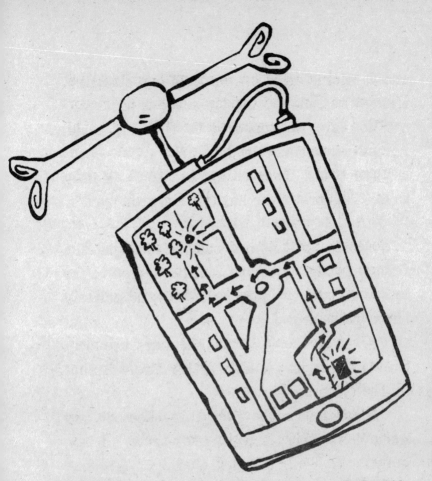

through a residential neighborhood filled with kids riding their bikes and playing ball in the street. (I think I recognize the ball as the All Ball, but I'm not sure.)

About five minutes later we enter a busy, crowded park. It's a beautiful, sunny Sunday and it seems as if everyone is out strolling, flying kites, picnicking—the place is packed!

"How are we supposed to find my math homework in this crowd?" I ask.

"Trust the Everything Locator," Manny says. "This prototype hasn't been wrong yet."

Yet?

I decide not to point out the fact that the first working prototype has been around for less than twenty-four hours. We wind our way through the crowd.

As we approach a group of benches, the locator starts beeping loudly. A tiny circle flashes on the screen.

"According to the Everything Locator, my math homework is right over there," I say, pointing to the bench just ahead.

This is weird. Did my math homework get up out of my backpack, walk around town for a few days, and then decide to take a stroll in the park?! Something is off. But what?

As we approach the bench from behind, I spot two girls sitting on it. The closer I get, the faster the circle on my phone flashes. I move close enough to look over the girls' shoulders. I see that one of them has a laptop. Looking more closely, I discover that the laptop is open to a website, and it's not just any old website—it's Tali DeCiso's website!

Tali DeCiso! The Italian art dealer? How can that be? This can't be a coincidence. The odds would be nearly impossible for some random stranger in the park to just happen to be looking at Tali DeCiso's website *and* have my math homework.

And that's when I see that she is not only looking at the site, but she is actively *editing* it! This girl is editing Tali DeCiso's website! Which means . . .

She might be Tali DeCiso!

I have to get a better look. Manny and I make our way around to the front of the bench. I'm ready to ask her what she's doing in town without telling my dad, or even ask why she needs my dad to move to Italy. All I know is that I need to talk to her. I get to the front of the bench, bracing myself, and look up.

I'm not face-to-face with Tali DeCiso.

I'm face-to-face with my inventing rival **NAT DEFINITE OF DEFINITE DEVICES!**

Chapter Ten

Home, Sweet Home

NEXT TO NAT DEFINITE SITS JADA PARIKH, HER business partner. Together, Nat and Jada run Definite Devices.

I am stunned. I don't have any idea what to say. In fact, I'm not even sure exactly what is going on here. None of this makes any sense. Tali DeCiso, Nat Definite, Jada Parikh, my missing math homework? What could these possibly have in common?

Manny is taken aback too. I think I even hear him gasp—which, if you know level-headed Manny, is big. Manny *never* gasps. But he recovers more quickly than me, and his mind works at the speed of light. It doesn't take him long to figure out what's going on here.

"You're Tali DeCiso!" Manny shouts at Nat. "Of course. I should have known!"

"What?!" I ask. "So there is no Tali DeCiso?"

Before anyone can say another word, I turn to Manny.

"How should you have known that Nat was really Tali?" I ask, still completely bewildered.

Manny pulls out his cell phone and goes to a translation app. "Look," he says. "'Deciso' means 'decided' in Italian—'decided' isn't so different from 'definite'!"

For some weird reason, in the middle of all this craziness, I think, *Emily could sure use that app.* Then I return to the situation at hand, and something else occurs to me.

Nat clearly did not expect Manny and me to find her. Her face turns pale.

"Um," she starts to say, but I jump in, her whole DIABOLICAL PLOT beginning to come clear.

"You tricked my dad into thinking you're some fancy art dealer! But you're not an art dealer at all. You're . . . you're . . ." I think about it for a second, getting madder and madder. "My dad is going to be really upset. He has his heart set on painting for Tali DeCiso, and now she doesn't even exist!"

Nat gets up from the bench and turns toward me.

"No, Billy, I really did offer your Dad a job!" she says. "And I *still am* offering him the job. His portraits are kind of kooky, but he's the *perfect* artist to help brand the next Definite Devices product, the FUNNY GUMMY!"

She takes out a zippered bag with what looks like sour gummy worms.

Jada—sensing this as some free publicity for their new product—says, "Here, take one. The Funny Gummy turns you into a funny guy for nine whole minutes, perfect for stand-up comedians and kids who want to impress their friends."

Manny shakes his head and waves her off.

Manny trained Jada on how to be a good CFO, so I think he feels a little responsible for her ill-timed eagerness.

"You have really terrible timing, Jada," I say, refusing to try the Funny Gummy.

Then I turn back to Nat.

"Why were you trying to make my dad move to Italy?" I ask her. "If you really want to hire him to paint, why can't he work for you here? And . . . while we're talking about strange stuff . . ." I glance at the Everything Locator. *"Why do you have my math homework?"*

Nat just looks down at her shoes. She doesn't say a word. Nobody does. Then she opens her bag, reaches in, and pulls out a piece of paper—MY MATH HOMEWORK!

She hands it to me, still not making eye contact.

Manny speaks up.

"Let me take a guess, okay? Nat has proven before that she'll do almost anything to work with me. So I'm going to guess that Nat tried to get your dad to move to Italy because I've made it clear that I'm not leaving Sure Things, Inc.

"But that doesn't mean that Nat isn't interested in joining *us* and working with me while you are away," Manny concludes.

I can't believe it! Could this whole thing just really be another plot to get Manny to work with her? I mean, I know Nat has a crush on Manny, but this is some really BAD STUFF.

Manny isn't finished.

"I think Nat snuck into World Headquarters after turning herself invisible with the Invisibility Spray and slipped your math homework out of your backpack to distract you from inventing while you looked for it.

"That way Sure Things, Inc. wouldn't have another successful invention, making her offer to work with me—which was sure to come after you left, Billy, if we hadn't found Clayton—more appealing. Wasn't that your thinking, Nat?"

Nat nods.

"It's true," she says. "Though I wouldn't be

too worried about the homework, Billy. Most of it was wrong anyway."

Wrong? I look down at the papers. It seems that Jada and Nat have corrected some of my numbers using a purple gel pen. I look closely at two or three of the answers they changed. In each case, they were right and I was wrong.

On second thought maybe I shouldn't hand this homework in to Mr. Kronod.

Nat continues. "And yes, Jada and I would love to be at Sure Things, Inc.—working with Manny, of course."

I realize at that moment that Jada hasn't said anything in a while. Something tells me she's not totally on board with this plan and is just going along because Nat said so.

So now what? Do I have to call Dad and tell him Tali DeCiso isn't real, or do I focus on the fact our biggest competitor has a really cool new invention, or . . . or . . .

And then the big takeaway really hits me.

"So, this means that the Sure family is NOT moving to Italy?" I say. I phrase it like a question, but it's definitely a statement.

"Well, not to work for Tali DeCiso, anyway," Nat says, flashing me a half smile.

"You know," I tell her, "as much as I really don't want to move to Italy, I also *really* don't want my dad to be disappointed. He was excited to be commissioned to paint. And he's going to very disappointed to learn that Tali DeCiso is a fake. After this, I highly doubt he'll agree to do the painting for the packaging of the Funny Gummy."

To my surprise, Nat looks genuinely upset.

"Does he have to know?" she asks. "I did go to his show at the art gallery, Billy. I thought it was cool. *Perfect* to help us design the Funny Gummy packaging and brand, and honestly, I'd really love to see what he can do. If you want, I can get in touch with him as Tali DeCiso and tell him that it's okay for him to work from home instead of Italy. We'll still pay him the same amount—minus the moving fees, of course."

This is a tough one. Once again Nat's plots

125

and lies have tricked us. How can we let this go again? I look over at Manny for advice.

"It's your decision, partner," he says, shrugging.

Bam!

Then I get an idea.

"All right, Nat. Here's what you've got to do if you *really* want Dad to work for you on this project," I begin. "One, you're going to tell him that Tali DeCiso doesn't need him to move to Italy but that she still wants him to work for her. You're right. There is no reason he has to know that Tali DeCiso isn't real.

"And two, you have to *double* your payment offer to him. That'll make him feel really good."

Jada opens the calculator app on her phone. Her fingers flash across the touch screen. She looks at Nat and she points to the screen.

"It's going to be tough, but we can swing that," she says.

Nat nods.

"One more thing," Manny adds. "Nat, you

have to promise that you'll never try to break up Sure Things, Inc. again. Same for you, Jada."

"I promise," Nat says immediately.

"Me too," says Jada. The four of us shake on it.

Then Jada, in true trained-by-Manny fashion, opens the zippered bag.

"Now would you try a Funny Gummy, Billy?" she asks sweetly.

I take a deep breath.

"Well, I guess if Dad is going to be involved with this invention, I might as well see if it works," I say.

I pop a Funny Gummy into my mouth. It tastes pretty much like regular gummy candy, only a little . . . funnier?

A few seconds later a joke pops into my head. From out of nowhere!

"Do you know what I would do if I saw Philo eating a dictionary?" I ask. No one replies. "I'd take the words right out of his mouth!"

I start giggling.

Am I the only one who thinks that's funny? Come on, that's FUNNY! Why is everybody groaning?

And then another joke pops into my head.

"What gets wet when it's drying?" I ask. Okay, this time no one is even trying to think about the answer. "A towel! Get it. A towel gets wet when it's drying. See?"

"Well, Billy, that's actually a riddle, not a jo-" Manny tries to stop me, but the jokes just keep on coming.

"Speaking of 'Billy,'" I say. "What belongs to you, but is used more by others? Your name!"

This is great stuff! What's wrong with everyone? Why aren't they laughing?

"Billy, I think we should call Clayton and fill him in on all this," Manny suggests.

"Sure," I say, whipping out my phone. I get Clayton on the line.

"Hey, Clayton, do you know what lawyers wear when they go to court?" I ask. "Lawsuits!"

"I think maybe I should handle this," Manny says, taking the phone from my hand. He leans over to Jada. "How long did you say the Funny Gummy lasts?"

"Nine minutes," Jada says.

Manny rolls his eyes. He fills Clayton in on what just happened, leading up to the fact that I'm not going to Italy after all.

"But we'd love it if you were a CONSULTANT FOR SURE THINGS, INC., Clayton," Manny tells him in a kind voice.

As it turns out, Clayton is actually relieved at this news!

"He says that your shoes are way too big for him to fill anyway," Manny says. Manny hands my phone back to me.

"And speaking of shoes," I say, thinking yet again of Dad, "What do you call a shoe that looks like a banana?" I see Nat and Jada giggle to each other. "A slipper! A *SLIPPER!*" I shout.

"Time to go home, Billy," Manny says.

In about two minutes and eighteen seconds, the Funny Gummy wears off, and I no longer find any of those jokes funny.

I arrive home a few minutes later. Dad is in the living room, practically jumping up and down from excitement.

"I just got a call from Tali DeCiso," says Dad. "She wants us to stay right here, but she still wants me to paint for her! And she's doubled her offer!"

Well, at least Nat was true to her word.

"That's wonderful news, Bryan!" says Mom, giving Dad a big hug. "Italy would have been fun, but this is our home."

Huh. For some reason, I'd never taken into account the fact that Mom and Dad would be sad to leave our house behind too. That kinda makes me feel a little better.

Only Emily is bummed out. Or, at least, I *think* she's bummed out. She's doing all her complaining in Italian—though I can't say I'm very surprised.

"This makes me so *giallo*," says Emily, stomping her foot.

"This makes you so *yellow*?" Dad asks. Then he shrugs it off.

"The Sure family is staying put," Dad says. "Right here in our own house."

I'm beaming. I can't believe that after all of this, I'm still going to get to work with Manny and get to be at Sure Things, Inc. All of this happiness is awesome.

"This house—that reminds me," Mom says suddenly, with a stern look on her face. "Billy, why is there a big PILE OF JUNK in the garage?"

Uh-oh!

Summer Vacation in the Sandbox

My name is Billy Sure. As of today, I can officially say I am no longer a seventh-grader at Fillmore Middle School. No, I'm not moving—though my family almost moved to Italy not too long ago (long story). I can say that because I'm now an eighth-grader at Fillmore Middle School!

Well, as my sister Emily might tell you, I'm not technically an eighth-grader yet, because it's still the summer before eighth grade, but I'm going to go ahead and call myself that anyway. You've got to celebrate the small things, right?

Anyway, it feels like just yesterday was the first day of seventh grade, when I went back to school after my first invention, the All Ball, went on sale. For as long as I can remember, I have always been coming up with invention ideas. It used to be a hobby, but together with my best friend Manny, we founded an invention company—Sure Things, Inc. I do the inventing, and Manny does the marketing, sales, and a whole lot of other cool stuff I don't really understand. That's how it's always been, and how it's always going to be!

Still, it's kind of crazy to think it's been almost a year since Sure Things, Inc. started. And it's also kind of crazy to think that today, summer vacation has started! Which means I can spend my days relaxing, taking my dog Philo on long walks, and, oh yeah, being a normal thirteen-year-old kid.

Just as I'm thinking about all of this, *Ping!* there's a notification on my laptop screen. I have an important e-mail to read.

Oh no, I think. I hope everything is okay with the Everything Locator. The Everything Locator is Sure Things, Inc.'s newest invention, and I think it's going to be our biggest hit yet.

I sign into my account and brace myself. But phew. The notification wasn't from Manny saying that our invention is doomed. It's from the makers of Sandbox, only the very best video game in the world!

Dear Billy Sure,
    Congratulations! You are now officially set up with a player account for Sandbox, everyone's favorite action-packed adventure. Please download the game at the link below. Have fun, and remember, in this game it's good to have your head in the sand!

Remember when I said I want to be a normal thirteen-year-old kid? Well, scratch that! I'm not a normal thirteen-year-old kid—I'm a thirteen-year-old kid with access to Sandbox!
    Yes!
    I've been on this video game's wait list for months, and I can't believe it's finally my time to play.
    Just as I download it and the game starts to install, I hear a voice from outside my door.
    "Billy!" says the voice.

That's my mom.

"Billy, have you finished unpacking?" Mom asks, peeking into my room.

I groan. Yeah, unpacking. Remember when I said that my family almost moved to Italy? Well, we cut it pretty close. My dad is an artist, and he was offered a job to do a series of paintings over there. We had everything packed and ready to go—until Manny and I discovered that the art dealer wasn't a real art dealer, she was actually the head of our rival invention company, Nat Definite, and it was all a ruse to get me out of the inventing biz! Thankfully we made a deal with her—she still had to commission Dad for some art, but he could do it right here at home. Case closed, right?

Not so much. Because thanks to Nat's alter ego, "Tali DeCiso," I now have a huge chore ahead of me—unpacking.

"I'll start that now, Mom," I say, looking sadly at my computer screen. How can my inventing rival still be messing up my life?

I spend some time emptying the last few

boxes and put stuff back where it belongs. My dog, Philo, curls up on a pile of stinky socks that I unpack. I'm not sure why the socks are stinky and I definitely don't understand why Philo wants to sleep on them. *Thanks for the help, Philo,* I think.

I go throughout the house putting things back, like my bathroom towels in the bathroom.

In the kitchen I see Dad's artist's lamp sitting on the counter in the exact spot where the blender should be. *So what's in Dad's art studio?* I think.

Curiosity gets the better of me and I head out of the house to his art studio, which is conveniently located in the garden shed.

Aha! Neatly poised above Dad's drawing board is the missing blender!

I guess Dad got a bit confused while he was unpacking. Oh boy!

I head into the house and back up to my room. As I pass the bathroom I see a spatula sitting in the toothbrush holder.

Oh no, I think, realizing Dad made breakfast

earlier today. *What did he use to cook with?*

Finally, after an hour of unpacking, I settle down in front of my computer and enter the world of Sandbox!

The game starts off simply enough. I get to create my avatar, which of course looks just like me only . . . Sandbox-like.

I build my house—which looks a lot like a medieval castle—and walk around until I run into a GIANT SAND MONSTER who charges right at me!!!

I race to the water and dive into the ocean. Knowing he will be instantly dissolved if he follows, the sand monster roars in anger, waving his dusty fist at me. Unfortunately, I know that the game won't let me stay in the ocean forever. After a few more seconds a giant wave approaches from behind.

If I stay in the water I'll get crushed by the wave. If I go back out onto the beach, the sand monster will get me. There's only one thing to do. I must control the huge wave of water and direct it onto the sand monster.

Just a video game, I remind myself. Nothing to be afraid of.

I start hitting the arrow keys on my keyboard, and I don't think my reflexes have worked this fast ever. Up, down, up, left, left, across, side—

I hardly notice the time, but suddenly two hours have passed.

"Billy! Dinnertime!" Dad calls from downstairs.

"I'm not hungry," I call back, pausing the game midbattle. I don't even want to imagine what toothbrush-infested food Dad has managed to cook up.

Then I hear my mom's voice.

"It's Chinese takeout," she calls.

Chinese takeout? Well, that's an eggroll of a different color. There are very few things more important than defeating a giant sand monster. Chinese takeout is one of them!

Leaving the game paused, I scramble downstairs. On my way to the kitchen I pass through the living room and see that the vacuum cleaner is sitting on the TV stand. I wonder where the TV could be?

Shrugging, I head to the kitchen and take a seat. Boxes of Chinese food are spread out across the table. I grab the biggest box, dump a huge helping of lo mein onto my plate, and start shoveling noodles into my mouth.

"I have to admit, I'm glad we didn't move to Italy," says Mom, pouring some wonton soup into a bowl. "Lots of lasagna, but we would have missed the food from here!"

I nod and moan my agreement, lo mein dangling from my mouth. Everyone looks at my older sister Emily, waiting for her to comment—something that is always unpredictable— but she says nothing.

"And I am completely unpacked!" Dad says proudly, dumping fried rice onto his plate.

I wonder if he knows just how bad of a job he did with the unpacking.

I reach in to grab an egg roll. That's when I realize that not only is Emily quiet, but she also hasn't had a single bite of food or even taken any to eat. Her plate is completely clean.

Of course, the less Emily eats, the more there is for me, but it's still weird since Emily loves Chinese food. She sits at the other end of the table, arms crossed in front of her. I wonder what she's grumpy about today.

"Come on, Em, at least try the lo mein," Mom says. "The noodles are soft."

Emily grunts but remains tight-lipped.

Maybe this is just Emily's latest "thing," I think. My sister is known for her "things." Let's see . . . some of Emily's things have including wearing glasses without lenses, speaking only in a British accent, painting each of her fingernails different colors, and her latest (before whatever this one is now) using random Italian words incorrectly when she thought we were all moving to Italy.

After my fourth helping of lo mein, I'm full. I help clear the table. When I'm done, I head upstairs to resume my game. It's time for level two where I'll have to defeat the EVIL SUPER SAND FLY STORM!

From the Sandbox to the Office

A huge wave slams me in the back of the head, knocking me down into the ocean. I'm completely underwater, yet somehow I can still breathe. A colorful tropical fish swims by and I pause to admire its beauty.

Just as I'm doing that, the fish turns into a shark. It races toward me with its mouth wide open!

Sandbox! I think. I'm just playing Sandbox. The shark is not real.

But wait! I'm in the game . . . not my avatar. And I'm about to be devoured by the shark!

I swim as fast I can away from the shark and back to the beach, which is when a giant sand monster sends me back into the water!

I'm going down . . . down . . . down. . . .

Until another colorful fish swims up to me and says, "It's only a game, after all."

A talking fish?! Something is wrong here.

And that's when I wake up.

I sit up in bed and discover that I'm still dressed in the clothes I wore yesterday. Next to my pillow is my laptop, with Sandbox on the screen. The theme music is still playing.

Okay, I know I only started yesterday, but I think it's already time for me to put the game away for a while.

I quickly shower, feed Philo, and grab some breakfast.

"Wanna go for a walk, buddy?" I ask Philo as he finishes his breakfast and licks the bowl clean.

Philo's ears perk up at the word "walk," and he scampers to the front door.

I head outside, hop on my bike, and take off on a morning ride. Philo trots beside me. I start to daydream . . . and wonder what would happen if right now a three-headed sand monster showed up!

Yeah . . . definitely a little too much Sandbox.

As we continue our walk, Ding! I get an incoming text from Manny.

HQ today?

I glance at Philo, who has just finished his business, and text back:

K. See ya in a few!

I stop at home for a brief second to tell Mom where I'll be and grab my laptop. Then I ride my bike to the World Headquarters of Sure Things, Inc.—a.k.a. Manny's garage.

When I get there, I hop off my bike and head inside. Philo follows me and immediately curls up in his doggy bed—just another day at the office for Philo.

"Thanks for stopping by, Billy," says Manny. Then he gets right down to business. "I've reviewed the sales figures for our inventions for the year so far, and come up with some pretty cool marketing strategies for all of our products, not just the new stuff. I'm talking about the All Ball, the Sibling Silencer, and all the others. We need to revamp all of our efforts across the board. You know, to remind people where it all started for Sure Things, Inc."

That's my friend Manny. I love his dedication, though sometimes I worry that he works too hard and doesn't have enough fun. Just don't tell him I think that!

"That all sounds great. But what do you need me for?" I ask.

"Well, I'm thinking this marketing strategy would be best launched alongside a new product," Manny begins.

Uh-oh, I know where this is going . . .

"So, even though it's summer vacation, I think we should start working on our Next Big Thing," says Manny, like coming up with a new invention is no big deal.

I grimace.

"I'm not really ready yet, Manny," I say, figuring he'll certainly understand. "I mean, you know how much I love inventing, but I don't want to feel pressured. We both worked really hard all school year, not to mention everything that's happened with Sure Things, Inc. I just want to chill. Play some Sandbox, ride my bike, you know. Just for a little bit."

This isn't the first time I've wanted to relax. But come on. This is summer vacation we are talking about!

Manny frowns, something he doesn't usually do.

"Billy, we can't just stop inventing over summer break. We're an invention company. That's what we do. We don't loaf around on the beach. We invent." Manny shakes his head and continues. "Companies always need new products. That's what being in business means. Customers and retailers have short memories. If we wait too long, we'll lose valuable retail space to other companies. And once that happens we may never get it back."

I don't know what to say. Manny knows a lot more about business than I do, so he's probably right about all this.

But also I really want a summer vacation. "Okay, Manny, just let me finish this level and then we'll talk about a new invention." I pull out my phone and start playing the mobile version of Sandbox.

But Manny isn't done yet.

"Billy, what's the point of playing that video game?" he asks. "Or any video game, really? Why pretend that you're doing something exciting when you can actually do something exciting, like invent a new product?"

A tense silence fills the room. I try to focus on my game, but I feel Manny staring at me.

"C'mon, partner," Manny says, breaking the silence. "Can't we think of something together? We always do."

I hear what Manny says, but I ignore him. Partly because I'm a little annoyed at how insistent he is. It's like he's not listening to what I have to say. And partly because I'm locked into Sandbox again, where I'm about to roll a giant ball of wet sand over an army of radioactive crabs. If I can destroy the creatures in the next ten seconds, I'll advance to the next level.

I steer the sloppy ball of sand toward the glowing red crabs, but they're cleverer than I thought. They form lines and start crawling in a bunch of different directions. My wet sand ball rolls right past them.

I want to make it to the next level, and I also really don't want to be having this conversation with Manny right now. As I plan my next attack against the crabs, **KER-BLAM!** A brilliant idea pops into my head!

"Why don't you invent something, partner?" I say, anxious to remain focused on the game. "Instead of staring at your spreadsheets all day?"

The running-out-of-time music starts playing. . . .

Within seconds, I'm surrounded. Mutant radioactive crabs rush at me from all sides. There's only one way out of this . . . and I take it. I dive into the water and begin my warrior's magic chant:

Ocean power within my hand, unleash your fury upon the sand!

A huge wave rises up, crashes onto the beach, and pulls all the radioactive crabs into the ocean.

Bing-boong! the game rings out, indicating that I have advanced to the next level. I press pause, then turn to Manny. And that's when it hits me.

Did I just tell Manny to invent?!

"All right," Manny replies calmly. "Maybe I will. Maybe you'll have to start calling me Manny Reyes, Kid Entrepreneur!"

He's not done yet.

"Actually, I think it's a great idea," he continues. "And you, Billy, can manage the business side, since you also enjoy staring at screens all day." He points to the screen on my phone, where giant jellyfish are starting to plan an attack against my avatar.

Manny is smiling, but I feel bad.

I can't believe I was so short with Manny. I really didn't mean to be, I think.

"Manny, I'm sorry," I say, putting my phone down. "I didn't mean to be so snappy with you. I was just so locked into the game."

Manny shrugs. "No, I'm not upset," he says. "I actually think that us switching roles is a pretty good idea. That way we can understand what we each do a little better. It can be a competition, a friendly switcheroo! You'll get to see what I do up close, and vice versa. Actually, I think it could be healthy for the company."

I wasn't really being serious when I said that Manny should invent something, but when Manny puts it that way, it actually might be a good idea.

And how hard can it be? Sure, Manny is a marketing and business genius, but marketing and selling a product can't be as tough as, I don't know, inventing one from nothing, right?

"Okay!" I say. "You're on! What invention will you be working on? Maybe you can invent a video game that kids can play while also letting them pay attention to other people."

(I really do feel bad about snapping at Manny.)

Manny smiles, letting me know that he realizes how terrible I feel. Reason #913 why I'm glad Manny is my best friend—we just get each other.

"Actually, I do have an idea for an invention," Manny says, turning serious.

"Already?" I ask, a bit shocked and a little jealous that Manny is able to come up with something so fast.

"Yup," Manny says. "And you're the one who inspired it. For my first invention as Manny Reyes, Kid Entrepreneur, I'm going to invent the Candy Toothbrush!"

DATE	ISSUED TO
1951	Matt Vezza
1977	Jada Reese
1696	Luis Ramirez

TIME MACHINES MAY BE HARD TO INVENT, BUT TIME TRAVEL STORIES AREN'T! GO BACK IN TIME ON HILARIOUS ADVENTURES WITH THE STUDENTS OF SANDS MIDDLE SCHOOL IN

IN DUE TIME

Did you LOVE reading this book?

Visit the Whyville...

IN THE MIDDLE BOOK HIVE

Where you can:

- Discover great books!
- Meet new friends!
- Read exclusive sneak peeks and more!

Log on to visit now!
bookhive.whyville.net

Whyville

a Numedeon, Inc. property